Parent's Introduction

Whether your child is a beginning reader, a reluctant reader, or an eager reader, this book offers a fun and easy way to encourage and help your child in reading.

Developed with reading education specialists, *We Both Read* books invite you and your child to take turns reading aloud. You read the left-hand pages of the book, and your child reads the right-hand pages—which have been written at one of six early reading levels. The result is a wonderful new reading experience and faster reading development!

You may find it helpful to read the entire book aloud yourself the first time, then invite your child to participate the second time. As you read, try to make the story come alive by reading with expression. This will help to model good fluency. It will also be helpful to stop at various points to discuss what you are reading. This will help increase your child's understanding of what is being read.

In some books, a few challenging words are introduced in the parent's text, distinguished with **bold** lettering. Pointing out and discussing these words can help to build your child's reading vocabulary. If your child is a beginning reader, it may be helpful to run a finger under the text as each of you reads. Please also notice that a "talking parent" ☺ icon precedes the parent's text, and a "talking child" ☺ icon precedes the child's text.

If your child struggles with a word, you can encourage "sounding it out," but keep in mind that not all words can be sounded out. Your child might pick up clues about a word from the picture, other words in the sentence, or any rhyming patterns. If your child struggles with a word for more than five seconds, it is usually best to simply say the word.

Most of all, remember to praise your child's efforts and keep the reading fun. After you have finished the book, ask a few questions and discuss what you have read together. Rereading this book multiple times may also be helpful for your child.

Try to keep the tips above in mind as you read together, but don't worry about doing everything right. Simply sharing the enjoyment of reading together will help increase your child's interest and skills in reading.

We Both Read: Oh, No! We're Doing a Show!

Text Copyright © 2011 by Dev Ross
Illustrations Copyright © 2011 by Meredith Johnson

We Both Read® is a trademark of Treasure Bay, Inc.

Published by
Treasure Bay, Inc.
P. O. Box 119
Novato, CA 94948 USA

Printed in Singapore

Library of Congress Catalog Card Number: 2011925872

PDF E-Book ISBN-13: 978-1-60115-547-4
Hardcover ISBN-13: 978-1-60115-255-8
Paperback ISBN-13: 978-1-60115-256-5

We Both Read® Books
Patent No. 5,957,693

Visit us online at:
www.webothread.com

PR-6-11

WE BOTH READ®

Oh, No!
We're Doing a Show!

By Dev Ross

Illustrated by Meredith Johnson

TREASURE BAY

Mrs. Carson is the best teacher in the world. She makes school fun. But Monday morning I did NOT have fun in Mrs. Carson's class. That's when she told us we were going to put on a talent **show**.

She said that we would all be in it. But I did not want to be in the **show**!

Mrs. Carson said that some **people** may want to sing or dance or play a musical instrument. Others may want to draw pictures or tell jokes or perform a science experiment. She said we should all do something that we like to do.

 I love to do ALL of those things. I just do not
like to do them in front of **people**!

My best friend, Pam, was very excited about the show. During recess, she told me, "Keesha! I'm going to do **something** great in the show. I'm going to *sing*! No, wait! I'll *dance*! No! I'll sing *and* dance!" Then she asked, "What are *you* going to do?"

I said I didn't know.

 "Never fear!" said Pam. "I will help you find
something to do. It will be fun!"

After school we went up to my room and closed the door. I didn't want my mom to see me practicing. I didn't want *anyone* to see me practicing!

A moment later, there was a tap on the door.

I didn't want to open it, but I did. I was glad that
it was just my dog, Jack.

Pam started twirling in front of my mirror. "Why don't you dance in the show?" she said as she twirled. "You're a very good dancer, Keesha." She pulled me to my feet, and we twirled together!

First my feet got mixed up in Pam's feet. Then Pam's feet got mixed up in mine.

Then Jack jumped in. We all fell down! It was funny, but I didn't want to do it in the show.

"Why don't you sing?" Pam suggested. "You know lots of songs!"

Pam was right. I do know lots of songs. **Listening** to music is one of my favorite things to do.

"Okay," I said. "Here I go!"

I started to sing, and I knew all the words! That's the good news.

I'm better at **listening** than I am at singing. That's the bad news.

Pam said everyone would be singing and dancing, and maybe I should try something different. I thought that was a good idea.

"You can stand on your head and recite a poem!" she suggested.

I put my head on the carpet. I put my feet over my head, and then . . . I felt **dizzy**.

My room was upside down. Pam was upside down. Jack was upside down! Being upside down did not feel good. It made me very, very **dizzy**.

I was getting very worried, but Pam had one more idea. "I know!" she said. "You can tell a joke! Do you know any funny ones?"

I told her the only joke I know.

 "Why do birds fly south for the winter?" I asked.

"I don't know," she said.

"Because it is too far to walk," I answered.

Pam laughed so hard that she fell right off her chair!

"That's perfect!" she said as she grabbed her backpack and headed for the door. "Now don't worry! You are going to be *great* in the show!"

I was happy that Pam liked my joke.

Then I thought about all the people at the show who would be watching me.

I wasn't so happy anymore.

The next morning, Mrs. Carson asked everyone to share what they were going to do for the show. Instantly my tummy felt strange. I tried not to think about being scared. I tried to think about my joke, but the more I tried, the more I could NOT **remember** it!

Was my joke about birds or bats? Did they fly or take a bus? Help! I could not **remember** my joke!

Lucky for me, Mrs. Carson picked Pam to go first. She ran to the stage, cleared her throat and began. She sang at the top of her voice! Her feet banged on the floor—TAP, TAP, TAP! It was so **loud** that we all had to put our fingers in our ears!

"That was very **loud**, Pam," said Mrs. Carson.
Pam smiled. "Thank you, Mrs. Carson!" Then
she sat down and looked over at me. "You're going
to be great too, Keesha!"

One by one Mrs. Carson called on the kids in my class to share their talent.

Nick spun a basketball on the tip of his finger. Brittany drew a picture of a horse. Liz twirled a hula hoop. Carlos poured vinegar into a volcano filled with baking soda. It **bubbled** and fizzed and flowed like lava!

 Sue was next. She put five sticks of **bubble**gum in her mouth. Then she blew a bubble. A big, BIG bubble!!

POP!!!

Finally I was the only one left to show my talent. Mrs. Carson turned to me and smiled. She was about to call my name when . . . RING! The lunch bell rang!

I was so happy that I did not have to tell my joke.
I was saved by the bell!

Then Mrs. Carson said, "Keesha, you can show us your talent right after lunch."

Suddenly I wasn't hungry anymore.

Lunchtime went by very fast. Pam said she could not wait to hear me tell my joke. I told her I could wait a long, long time.

The lunchbell rang, and we went back to the **stage** in the
auditorium. I knew Mrs. Carson was going to call on me,
so I tried to hide behind my math book. It didn't work. She
called on me anyway.

I walked up to the **stage**. I looked out at all of the
kids. All of the kids looked at me. My tummy hurt
and I felt dizzy.

Mrs. Carson could see that something was wrong. "Are you okay, Keesha?" she asked in a gentle voice.

I turned to her, trying very hard not to cry. "I'm sorry, Mrs. Carson," I said. "I don't want to be in the talent show."

I told her I did not like to do things in front of people. I said it made my tummy hurt to think about it.

"You don't like to perform?" Mrs. Carson asked in surprise.

I shook my head and looked at the floor. Was Mrs. Carson mad at me? Was I in trouble?

"Well, if you don't like to perform, we'll just have to find something else for you to do, Keesha," she said. "You can help **backstage**."

 "**Backstage**?" I asked.

Mrs. Carson smiled and nodded. "No one can see you when you are back there!"

 I smiled back at Mrs. Carson. "I would LOVE to help backstage!"

Mrs. Carson explained that I would be helping the other kids in my class get ready for the show. And that's just what I did.

I helped paint the set. I helped Liz make a skirt. I put all of the props in one place. (A prop is what people carry on stage with them.)

The day of the show arrived, and the audience was full! We were just about ready to start when Nick's basketball went flat. Then Liz's grass skirt tore. And Carlos spilled his vinegar! "Don't worry," I said with a grin. "I'm here to help!"

The show was a big hit. All of the people there loved it. They clapped and cheered. It was a wonderful sound.

After it was over, Mrs. Carson stepped out onstage and thanked the audience for coming to the show. She thanked the children for doing such a wonderful job performing. All of the performers took a **bow**.

Then she thanked *me* for my work backstage!

"Will you come out and take a **bow** too,
Keesha?" she asked.

I did—and I even felt good in front of all
those people!

If you liked *Oh, No! We're Doing a Show!*, here is another
We Both Read® book you are sure to enjoy!

A Pony Named Peanut

Jessica's mother has sent her to spend the summer with her aunt and uncle in the country. Jessica doesn't think that living on a farm, far from a city, will be any fun at all. At first, she hates life in the country, but then she meets a special pony that has been rescued from an animal shelter. Slowly, she begins to think that this summer might not be so bad after all. Now, if only that boy, Max, would stop making fun of her . . .

To see all the We Both Read books that are available,
just go online to **www.WeBothRead.com**.